DIARY OF A Soccer Star

Shamini Flint

Illustrated by Sally Heinrich

ALLEN&UNWIN
SYDNEY·MELBOURNE·AUCKLAND·LONDON

This edition published in 2012

First published in Singapore in 2010 by Sunbear Publishing

Allen & Unwin
83 Alexander Street
Crows Nest NSW 2065
Australia
Phone: (612) 8425 0100
Fax: (612) 9906 2218
Email: info@allenandunwin.com
Web: www.allenandunwin.com

A Cataloguing-in-Publication entry is available
from the National Library of Australia
www.trove.nla.gov.au

ISBN 978 1 74237 825 1

Text design by Sally Heinrich
Cover design by Jaime Harrison
Set in 10/14 pt Comic Sans

This book was printed in May 2016 at McPherson's Printing Group,
76 Nelson St, Maryborough, Victoria 3465, Australia.
www.mcphersonsprinting.com.au

20 19 18 17 16 15

MY SOCCER DIARY

I scored a goal today.
Unfortunately, it was an *own* goal.
It wasn't my fault.
Really, it wasn't!

Jack 'Talk to the Feet' Gordon hit the ball back
to the keeper. (I've just found out this is called
a back pass.)

The goalkeeper went for one of those long kicks...
why couldn't he just pick the ball up, the clod?

(I've just discovered that the goalie is not allowed
to pick the ball up from a back pass – stupid rule!)

You see, the coach had told
me to play in defence...

So what actually happened
was that the ball hit me
on the back.

Well, to be honest,
the ball hit
my bottom...

I scored an own goal.

I scored an own goal with my BOTTOM!

I SCORED AN OWN GOAL WITH MY BOTTOM!!!

Does life get any worse than that?

YES – if some smart alec with his dad's iPhone took a photo at exactly that moment and sent it to the school newspaper.

Time to spend an awful lot of time in my room with a paper bag over my head.

My name is Marcus (no, you may not call me Mark) Atkinson and I am nine years old.

There are two things I need to be absolutely clear about:

I don't want to play soccer.

I don't want to keep a diary.

In fact, you could say that I don't want to KEEP A DIARY ABOUT PLAYING SOCCER!!!

But Dad says that WRITING DOWN MY GOALS will help me achieve them.

Yeah right!

Actually, I did try Dad's stupid plan.

I didn't want to miss out if there was something in this 'writing it down will make it happen' stuff.

I wrote down:

I would like to win $1,000,000 in the lottery.

I would like JT (the school bully) to leave me alone.

I would like Dad to give up trying to make me play soccer.

Well, that DIDN'T work.

So now I just write down whatever I feel like about Dad and JT and everyone else who's on my case –

and I keep the diary

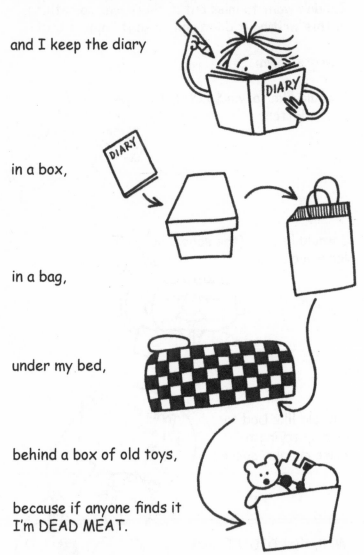

in a box,

in a bag,

under my bed,

behind a box of old toys,

because if anyone finds it I'm DEAD MEAT.

My dad is always trying to persuade people that they can

work harder…

run faster…

climb higher…

You get the picture.

He's even written a book called
Pull Yourself Up by Your Own Bootstraps!

I had to explain to him that it isn't even possible to do that. How dumb is Dad?

(But people still buy the book, so maybe Dad isn't so dumb after all.)

Dad says, 'Success is a state of mind.'

There's a lot of stuff like that in his book.
This is from Chapter 2.

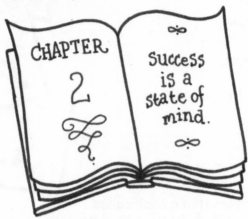

If I wrote a book it would say,
'SUCCESS is not scoring a goal with your
BOTTOM' or 'SUCCESS is not having to wear a
PAPER BAG on your head'.

That's why I haven't written a book and I don't plan to write a book and I DON'T WANT to write this diary!

But Mrs Abraham, my teacher, told Mum that I need to practise my spelling and punctuation.

In kes youre wandering why this diery has no mistaiks its beecoz my sista Gemma found it and fixd everifing

My problems started when Dad decided that I needed to be a TEAM PLAYER.

(Dad is the only person I know who can speak in capital letters.)

He decided that I needed more FRIENDS.

He decided that I spent too much time on my Nintendo DS.

SO Dad told me I had to join a soccer team.

THAT was officially the worst day of my life EVER!

And in case you think I'm kidding, it was WORSE than when:

JT (the school bully) tipped my food tray in my lap,

JT gave me a wedgie in front of all the girls,

JT made a paper aeroplane out of my maths homework.

(Well, that was the worst day of my life EVER until today when I scored the own goal with you-know-what.)

to goal

ball

bottom

The problem is that I'm not very good at sport – ANY sport.

I can prove it:

When I was three years old – I came last in an egg-and-spoon race...

When I was four – I came last in a sack race...

When I was five – I was last in a three-legged race...

Graham – the kid who was tied to me – hasn't spoken to me since.

When I was six, I was picked last for a running race – after all the GIRLS!

I stopped PLAYING ANYTHING.

And now Dad wants me to play SOCCER.

Yeah – by scoring own goals with my bottom!

Yeah – by hiding in my room with a paper bag over my head!!

Yeah – just remember that newspaper article!!!

Even my best friend, James Carville, sniggered when someone called me Marcus 'Talk to the Bottom' Atkinson.

And he's the class nerd.

James can do the Rubik's Cube in fifteen seconds.

I can do it in fifteen minutes – by taking the stickers off the cubes and moving them around OR by dismantling the whole thing.

Dad came up with a strategy for my soccer career.

'Everything in life needs a strategy.' (Chapter 14 of the *Bootstraps* book)

THE STRATEGY – JOIN A SOCCER TEAM

Dad tried to find a team for me...

The school team said 'no thank you' thirty seconds into my trial.

The park team said, 'No way!'

Mum's office kids' team said, 'In your dreams...'

(Well, they didn't actually say that, but I could guess that's what they were thinking.)

'If the strategy isn't working, change the strategy.' (Chapter 8 of THAT book)

Dad decided to PAY for SOCCER TRAINING!

I am just gutted when I think of all the stuff
we could have spent the money on...

Soccer training is NOT fun.

There are five other boys and one girl in the same boat as me.

Except they seem happy to be there.

Three of the boys are Manchester United supporters, one Chelsea and one Arsenal.

They're all much better than me – even the girl whose name is Lizzie.

(She supports Liverpool and is in a bad mood about it because they hardly ever win anything anymore.)

All the others call Liverpool 'Loser-pool'. He-he! I think it's quite funny too.

Hee!
He-he-hee!
Hee! Hee!
Hee!

Then one of the others asked me which team
I supported.

I panicked and couldn't remember any team names.

I don't know why I was trying to talk to the kids
anyway. They all speak funny.

Drog – what?

He's a screamer? Even I
don't do that at soccer –
not often anyway.

Back heel? They play with their heels?

Who are they trying to call 'On-ree'? Just call him Henry like everyone else!

Later Dad told me:

- Didier Drogba plays for Chelsea.
- A screamer is a shot on goal that's struck very hard.
- Using the back of the heel is a skill.
- Henry is French and that's how you're supposed to say his name. Yeah – whatever. And he cheated and scored a goal with his hand. Dad must be out of his mind. What kind of role model is that for a child?
  For me?
  Does he want me to learn how to cheat??

Map of the World

Where is Slovenia and why would anyone want to draw it?
Translation: Slovenia is in England's group in the World Cup and might be quite hard to beat.

Back to soccer training –

You pass using the side of your foot.

pass with this bit

You shoot using your bootlaces.

shoot from here

Here's the deal – I can only just about manage to tie my shoelaces.

I still have to say 'one loop, two loops, twist, through the hole, pull' in a whisper with my tongue sticking out of the corner of my mouth when I do it.

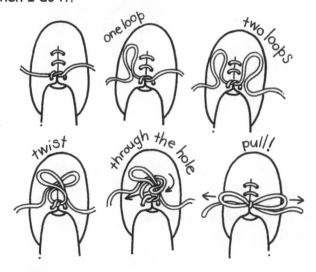

What are the chances I can SCORE A GOAL with my bootlaces?

The kids kept saying strange things like, 'Ronaldo can move the ball both ways from a free kick'. Should I have told them that 'nothing in life is free'? (Chapter 7 of *Bootstraps*.)

This is what it actually means.

The coach told us to turn with the ball. It made me dizzy.

It made me even dizzier to watch Jack 'Talk to the Feet' Gordon do it.

Coach asked us to skip on and off the ball.

Do I look like a circus elephant?

And then we were invited to play a match against a park side.

The other kids were hopping up and down with excitement.

I was DEVASTATED.

I hadn't even learnt to play yet!
I thought this was supposed to be training?

Train smart, not hard.

(Has the coach been reading Dad's book??)

Well, the rest, as they say, is history.

to goal

ball

bottom

I now OFFICIALLY have the most famous bottom in school.

More famous than the bottoms of:

Frederick Wrenthorpe – who was bitten by the school cat.

Famous bottom #1

Famous bottom #2

Joshua Day – who got too close to a Bunsen burner (he needed skin grafts).

Famous bottom #3

Henry (not On-ree) Halliday – who got stuck in a revolving door (it's all about timing, getting through one of those).

I need a magic spell to make me invisible.

Since I don't have one of those, I begged Dad to let me give up soccer instead.

Never give up! Never give in!

He sounds like his book even when he isn't reading out loud from it.

At the next training lesson, the kids still hadn't stopped laughing at my bottom goal.

The coach asked everyone to head the ball to each other.

The kids played bottom ping-pong instead.

We moved on to the next drill – we practised step-overs.

Or at least the others practised step-overs.

I practised step-ons, step-ins and step-arounds.

I also practised the sit-down and the fall-down...

The others played more bottom ping-pong.

Lizzie took pity on me.

I stayed silent.

I think I made her nervous by mentioning Dad's book because she skipped away.

She did a triple
step-over on the way.

It looked so easy when she did
it. So I tried again.

I did my special 'stand-on,
fall-over'.

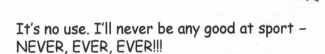

It's no use. I'll never be any good at sport –
NEVER, EVER, EVER!!!

I'm actually quite good at maths.

We did fractions today.

If I spent 1/2 the time doing stuff that Dad makes me do I would be 2x as happy.

If 1/10 of the kids in school didn't see the school newspaper article about my own goal, and there are 100 kids in school – 10 would not be laughing at me.

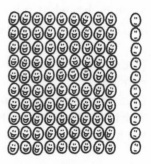

If JT would spend 2/3 of his time bullying one of the other kids, only 1/3 of his time would be spent bullying ME!

JT is hopeless at maths.

I'm gonna break you in half, Marcus. And then I'm going to kick all three pieces around the park...

Yeah right, what a loser.
You'll only have two pieces to kick around, so there!

(I don't say this out loud, of course – I'm too busy running.)
Chapter 14 of *that* book – 'Never run away from a fight.' Dad has never met JT or he wouldn't write such stuff.

Besides, it doesn't really make a difference if I'm in two pieces or three.

I'd rather be in
1=2/2=3/3=4/4=5/5=6/6
pieces.
So there!

1=2/2=3/3=4/4=5/5=6/6

Every day this week, I tried something different to get out of soccer.

On Monday, I held the thermometer under the hot water tap in the kitchen and showed Dad how ill I was.

Perhaps I shouldn't have added that last line. Anyway, it didn't work.

On Tuesday, I pretended to have a stomach-ache. Dad gave me the nastiest medicine I've ever tasted in my life.

I had to get better immediately.

On Wednesday, I arranged myself at the bottom of the stairs.

(Dad shouldn't be so cunning.)

On Thursday, I asked Mum for help.

She tried.

Dad went into full *Bootstraps* mode.

Mum never had a chance.

On Friday, I tried stealth mode. I decided to pretend to go to soccer practice and then hide out behind the gym.

I offered to *walk* to soccer. Usually, I insist on taking the car everywhere and it makes Dad mad.

Dad smelt something fishy.

Nightmare!!!

I swear I will never try and get out of soccer training again.

Dad watched my last training session.

Lizzie said 'Hi' to me.

Dad gave me the thumbs-up. He probably thinks I've made a friend.

If only he knew – a girl who plays soccer is feeling sorry for me...

The coach was being mysterious again.

I was sure I could do that. I have two feet!

(Later Dad told me that it means being able to kick the ball with either foot. Great – I'm not two-footed, I'm no-footed.)

Today, however, is not the worst day of *my* life.

It's the worst day of the life of some kid called Sebastian.

Sebastian's dad brought him for soccer training.

Sebastian is short and has spiky hair, freckles, glasses and a tummy like Uncle Joe 'Six-pack' Flint.

He had a book under one arm as if there would be time for reading during water breaks or something.

Who is he KIDDING?

Sebastian had to partner me because we're both new.

(Chapter 19, *Bootstraps* –
'Know your opponent's weaknesses.')

Sebastian made me look good.

Okay, he didn't make me look good.

But he did distract the coach...usually he's yelling at me. Not anymore!

I had no idea what the coach was muttering about but later Dad explained that the others were all great Brazilian soccer players.

At dinner that evening, Dad told Mum that parents who tried to turn their children into something they were not were really sad.

What's the weather like on your planet, Dad?

Good news and bad news.

Actually, good news and the WORST NEWS EVER!!!

GOOD NEWS

There is an inter-school maths competition and
Mrs Aziz asked me whether I would like
to take part.

Would I? Just fractions
and decimals
and multiplication...

No step-overs and
back heels and
turns that make me dizzy.

WORST NEWS EVER!!!

The soccer coach has signed us up for a mini-
soccer tournament.

Will he never learn?
Has he forgotten
THAT goal already?

Today, Coach was even weirder than usual. Maybe knowing we have a tournament has scrambled his brain.

Perfect dummies?? Maybe he was talking to Sebastian???

Later Dad told me a dummy is when you pretend to play the ball but don't, to fool the defender.

The next lesson was tackling.

Basically, if a player has the ball, you just run up and take it off him.

How hard can that be?

At least the maths competition is going well.

I've reached the semifinals.
I answered nine out of ten questions correctly on shapes.

The soccer competition is going well too. It's six-a-side, which means that Sebastian and I get to be in the reserves.

Coach only sends us on when the score is already around 12-0 so we can't do too much damage.

Dad is very disappointed. He wants me to 'seize the moment'.

Seize the moment!

I am, Dad. I'm seizing the moment not to make a complete idiot of myself.

Training has got worse. The coach really, really wants us to win the tournament. He needs to get a life.

Or maybe he thinks that he'll get a contract managing a really big team like the Chicago Bulls!

Dad explained to me later that the Chicago Bulls are a basketball team. Whatever.

I support Loser-pool. What do I know about soccer teams?

Dad really, really wants us to win the tournament too. He needs to get a life and STOP LIVING MINE!!!

Sit-ups, push-ups, laps, star jumps – this fitness training is going to be the end of me.

Besides, I need to practise my maths. The semifinal is on measurements, my weakest area.

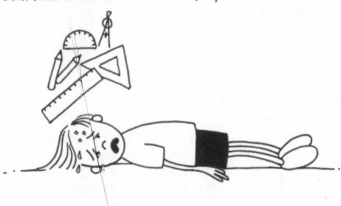

The maths semifinal was tough.

It came down to the last question.

Me against this kid from Portsdown Road School.

Whoever was first to the buzzer...

James had come along to support me. We're friends again even though he sniggered at my bottom goal.

Sebastian was there as well.

Although I'm not sure he was paying attention.

Lizzie came too.
She was wearing her Liverpool shirt.
Doesn't she have any other clothes?

The question:

A soccer team just won a semifinal, and the players are congratulating each other. If a player shakes hands with every other player on their own team, what is the total number of handshakes?

What?

What??

WHAT???

Not more soccer!

But wait a second...

I got it!

I'm right!!

I'm in the final...

The soccer semifinal was easy.

I came on as a defender when we were 7–0 up.

The other team scored four goals.

We still won 7–4.

That's when I discovered that the maths final and the soccer final were on the same day.

I looked at the kick-off times:

SOCCER FINAL: 2pm–3pm
MATHS FINAL: 3.15pm–4.15pm

THERE IS NO WAY I'M GOING TO GET FROM THE GAME TO SCHOOL ON TIME!!!

Not even if I have a bicycle

...or a personal rocket pack

...or superpowers!

I'm going to have to tell Dad...

No way!

I'm really going to have to tell Dad...

Nope.

Gotta do it...

Can't.

I'm STUFFED.

I was sitting in my room with the paper bag over my head again when I saw Dad's book.

I flipped through the pages.

CHAPTER 22

HAVE COURAGE! ☺

Okay.

58

What's with Dad?

I asked Mum.

Really?

Wow! Parents sure are weird.

We practised passing today.

It sounds easy, but whenever I try to pass the ball it either ends up behind the other player or too far in front.

Mind you, at least I'm not dangerous.

You should have seen what Jack 'Talk to the Feet' Gordon did to Sebastian...

That must have REALLY hurt.

The coach went ballistic. But he wouldn't stop practice. It got even more complicated.

We had to pass – and then run into SPACE.

run into space?

Yeah right. If I could do that, would I be hanging around some dumb soccer practice?

Later Dad explained that it meant to run into a section of the field where there were no players from the other team to receive a return pass.

PASS

run into space

DEFENDER

I should have guessed that. DUH!

But then Coach told us that if we couldn't pass we should just DRIBBLE down the pitch.

No way!

Only my little sister, Harriet, still dribbles and she's only nine months old.

And Mum wipes her chin with a cloth.

Does the coach want all the mums to come to the game with wet towels for their dribbling kids??

Coach said that we had to make sure we BEAT the other players *especially* ONE on ONE.

I am not going to get into a fight. Especially not one on one. Some of the other kids are MASSIVE.

Besides, I don't need my face mashed just before the maths final.

Dad explained afterwards that dribbling means running with the ball under control.

Beating players means going past them.

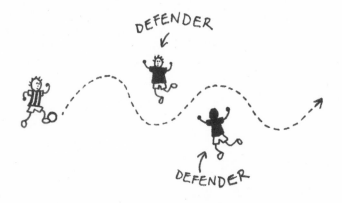

I don't need soccer boots to play soccer.

I need a DICTIONARY.

The maths final is on SHAPES and ANGLES.

Jack 'Talk to the Feet' Gordon says,
'Shapes and Angels?'

That's right, Jack. You just keep thinking with
your feet.

Obviously, I didn't say that out loud.
I'm not DUMB.

Tomorrow is the soccer final and the maths final.

Today is a day to rest.

So, you guessed it, Coach organised a training session.

What happened to 'work smart, not hard'?

Now, it's 'work until your legs fall off'??
That's not in Dad's book.

The practice session was – big surprise –
A DISASTER.

Even the kids who knew what they were
doing were rubbish.

Nerves, I guess.
Or butterflies...

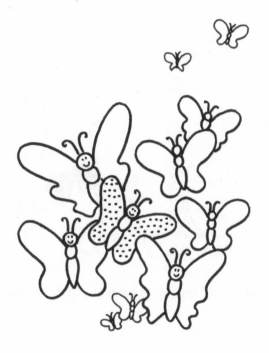

I have two finals tomorrow so I have a SWARM of
butterflies in my tummy.

Lizzie was acting really odd as well. She's usually the normal one.

She kept shouting 'SQUARE, SQUARE!' at me during practice.

Maybe she was trying to help me with my maths?

It's the end of the world as we know it.

Coach just called.

Jack 'Talk to the Feet' Gordon tripped over his shoelaces and broke his leg. He can't play in the final.

Sebastian refuses to play because of the knock he got last week.

Besides, he doesn't really play, does he?

I'm in...

I'm in the team.

I'M IN THE TEAM!

I'M IN THE TEAM AND WE'RE GOING TO LOSE!!

WE'RE GOING TO LOSE AND I'M GOING TO SCORE AN OWN GOAL!!!

I'M GOING TO SCORE AN OWN GOAL WITH MY BOTTOM!!!!

Dad's going to get mad and he won't take me to the maths final.

It's finals day and Dad is really excited.

He thinks it's time for me to 'step up'.

Haven't we had this conversation before?

The butterflies are
attacking my brain.

Even if I get to the maths final, I won't be able to
answer any questions on SHAPES and ANGLES.

I kan here Dad yelling from downstares.

GUD BYE DIERY –
I MAY NOT BE
ABEL TO TELL
YOU WAT HAPPEND.

All the way in the car, Dad kept saying things like:

Dad, you need to GET REAL. I'm Marcus 'Talk to the Bottom' Atkinson and I'm replacing Jack 'Talk to the Feet' Gordon.

I didn't say that aloud. You gotta let a man have his dreams...

When we got to the pitch I saw that the rest of the team were as depressed as me.

Only Lizzie tried to be nice.

Somehow that only made me feel worse. Especially since we both knew it wasn't true.

It was time.

We wore red stripes. They wore blue.
Two halves. Twenty minutes each way. Six-a-side.

The game kicked off.

Some kid in a blue
shirt ran past me
and scored.

Some other kid
in a blue shirt
ran past me and
scored.

The coach was shouting…

Lizzie managed to score one in return.

The ball hit me on the hand –
PENALTY!

I tried not to
look at Dad.

Half-time!

We sat by the side of the pitch.

Coach was yelling so loudly I couldn't hear him anymore.

Lizzie said:

It wasn't your fault really.

Yeah right.

At least you haven't scored a goal with your bottom yet.

I suddenly realised she was right. There was a funny side to this whole soccer thing. After all, it was just a game.

I looked at Coach.
His face was red.

I looked at Dad.
His face was red.

I felt like shouting, 'It's just a GAME!'

I didn't. I'm not THAT dumb. Coach would have attacked me with a corner flag.

Instead, I asked Lizzie why she had been shouting 'SQUARE, SQUARE,' at me the whole time.

She took a twig and drew a diagram on the ground.

'It means you have to pass ACROSS the pitch, not down the LINE.'

I looked at the diagram and realised something ENORMOUSLY IMPORTANT.

SOCCER was just like MATHS!
SOCCER WAS JUST LIKE MATHS!!!!

Soccer was just like maths except you had to do the sums with your FEET.

NO problem.

The whistle blew.

We were back on the pitch.

The score was still

Lizzie shouted SQUARE and I slid the ball sideways. She scored.

I shouted HYPOTENUSE but no one understood.

I shouted DIAGONAL and one of my team-mates slid the ball to me along the diagonal.

I scored. (First time ever with my *foot* – I didn't dare look at Dad in case he'd had a heart attack.)

I scored again!!

Lizzie asked me what a hypotenuse was as we jogged back to the centre.

She looked at me as if I was mad for knowing something like that.

But when we kicked off she shouted 'hypotenuse' and I slid the ball along the longest side of a right-angled triangle – obviously.

She scored!
5-6!
The final whistle blew!

Time to enjoy the VICTORY!!

Except that Dad grabbed my shoulder.

I had almost forgotten, can you believe it?

We got there just in time ...

ENUFF said – compared to soccer, maths is EASY!!

Dad sure was HAPPY! (Me too.)

Time for some well-deserved REST.

HELP!!! Dad's just told me I have to learn to play CRICKET!

About the Author

Shamini Flint lives in Singapore with her husband and two children. She is an ex-lawyer, ex-lecturer, stay-at-home mum and writer. She loves soccer!

www.shaminiflint.com

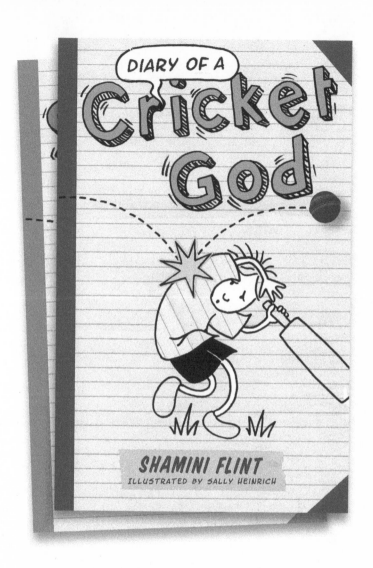

Now read my
Cricket Diary!